BOX

BBC CHILDREN'S BOOKS
UK | USA | Canada | Ireland | Australia
India | New Zealand | South Africa

BBC Children's Books are published by Puffin Books,
part of the Penguin Random House group of companies whose
addresses can be found at global.penguinrandomhouse.com.

www.penguin.co.uk
www.puffin.co.uk
www.ladybird.co.uk

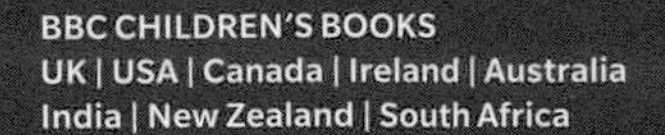

Penguin
Random House
UK

First published 2018
001

Illustrations:
Pages 6–13 and 39–44: comic illustrations by John Ross,
comic colours by James Offredi

Written by Paul Lang

Printed in Italy

A CIP catalogue record for this book is available from the British Library

ISBN: 978-1-405-93376-6

All correspondence to:
BBC Children's Books
Penguin Random House Children's
80 Strand, London, WC2R 0RL

CONTENTS

Watch out for this symbol! Every time you complete a Time Trial Mission, you'll be one step closer to saving the Doctor. Hurry – before the bad guys get to her first!

WHERE'S THE DOCTOR? PART 1

YOU KNOW WHERE SHE IS?
NOT QUITE. LONG-RANGE INTERSTELLAR SCANS CAPTURED HER FALLING TO EARTH.
WE THOUGHT SHE WAS DEAD, WHICH WOULD HAVE SUITED ME FINE.

BUT WE STARTED TO PICK UP ENERGY TRACES. MULTIPLYING. ONE TIME, ONE PLACE, ONE DAY.

SECOND OF JUNE 1953. LONDON.
THE CORONATION OF QUEEN ELIZABETH II.

JUST THE THREE MILLION PEOPLE LINING THE STREETS, THEN.
NO PROBLEM. ANYTHING ELSE I SHOULD LOOK OUT FOR?

YES. THE BLUE BOX. THE TARDIS. SHE TRAVELS IN IT, THROUGH TIME AND SPACE.
FIND IT AND YOU FIND HER.
POLICE BOX

DON'T WORRY. THIS THING WILL LEAD ME TO WHEREVER SHE IS.
BE DISCREET.
AND CLEAN UP ANY TRACE OF EXTRATERRESTRIAL ACTIVITY. BAD FOR BUSINESS.

BEEP!
BEEP!
BEEEEEEP!
THIS IS TOO EASY. I'LL JUST WAIT HERE FOR HER.

WAIT . . . WHAT?
QUICKLY, CHILD!
GRANDFATHER, IT'S COMING!

WE MUST PROTECT HER MAJESTY!
HER MAJESTY WILL BE FINE. WE HAVE TO GO!

NO EXTRATERRESTRIAL ACTIVITY, HE SAID.
I'D BETTER CLEAN THIS UP.

GET OUT OF HERE. *NOW!*
THANK YOU, MY DEAR! COME ALONG, SUSAN!

WAOH-WAOH-FZZZZZZZTTTTTTT
STRANGE. SHE WAS DEFINITELY HERE A MINUTE AGO.
I MUST HAVE MISSED HER WHILE I WAS DEALING WITH THAT . . . THING. SHE'S SLIPPED INTO THE CROWD.

SOON, OUTSIDE BUCKINGHAM PALACE . . .
BEEP! BEEP!
GOT THE SIGNAL AGAIN. FROM THAT ROW OF GUARDS.

THAT THING WILL NEVER SPOT US IN THIS GET-UP.
DOCTOR, WHERE'S YER TROOSERS?
OH, MY GIDDY AUNT! I DIDN'T GET THEM ON IN TIME.

ANOTHER ALIEN! MY SENSORS MUST BE PICKING IT UP, TOO.

PROBABLY AFTER THE DOCTOR AS WELL.
NO CHANCE, DEAR. THAT BOUNTY IS MINE!

HSSSSSSSS!
IT'S THE DEVIL BEASTIE!
WHEN I SAY 'RUN', RUN.
RUUUUUUN!

HOW MANY MORE OF THESE IDIOTS MUST I DEAL WITH?
I THINK SHE WENT THAT WAY.
BEEP! BEEP!

YOUR MAJESTY! I HAVE A GIFT FOR YOU!

WOULD YOU CARE FOR A JELLY BABY?
OH, PERHAPS NOT.
BUT IT'S DETECTING THE DOCTOR! IS THIS THING WORKING?

BRAVE HEART, TEGAN.

A SUITE AT THE RITZ! THE ONLY PLACE TO WATCH A CORONATION.
I CAN'T SEE A THING!

CHECK. MATE.
YOU HAVE DEFEATED ME. I WILL LEAVE THIS REALM.
WICKED!

FANTASTIC!

SHOULDA WATCHED IT ON THE TELLY!
NOT ANOTHER ONE!

CROWNS ARE COOL!

SO WHAT DO YOU THINK?
HMM. I PREFERRED VICTORIA'S.

4.30 P.M. THE MALL

I AM QUEEN ELIZABETH THE SECOND, AND YOU . . .

. . . ARE DISMISSED.

I'VE HAD ENOUGH OF THIS.
PATCH ME THROUGH TO THE CEO.
LOOK FOR THE DOCTOR YOURSELF.
I CAN'T FIND HER ANYWHERE.

EVENTUALLY . . .
COLBY! DISCONNECT HER.
HOLD ON. WHAT'S THAT? ZOOM IN!

TO BE CONTINUED!

The FIRST DOCTOR

The First Doctor might have looked like an old man, but he was actually the youngest of them all! He was practically a teenager compared to the Doctor we know now.

He left his home planet, Gallifrey, because he was bored with life there and wanted to explore the universe!

To do this, he stole a TARDIS – an incredible ship that travels in time and space, and can change its shape to blend in to any environment.

Most people thought this Doctor was very rude when they first met him, but he was secretly mischievous and funny.

HAVE YOU EVER THOUGHT WHAT IT'S LIKE TO BE WANDERERS IN THE FOURTH DIMENSION?

He dressed in very old-fashioned clothes and had long white hair.

ENEMY FILE: *the* DALEKS

WHO WERE THEY?

Super-mutated humanoids inside a mini-tank with loads of weapons and defence systems.

WHERE WERE THEY FROM?

Skaro, in the Seventh Galaxy.

WHAT DID THEY WANT?

To wipe out every other creature that exists! They thought they were the ultimate species, and didn't want to share the universe.

WHAT HAPPENED WHEN THE DOCTOR MET THEM?

He and his friends teamed up with the Thals, who also lived on Skaro. They raided the Dalek city and cut off its power supply, deactivating the lot of them!

◇ Susan was a pupil at Coal Hill School in 1963, but two of her teachers thought there was something a bit weird about her.

◇ So they followed her home, which turned out to be a strange blue box called the TARDIS, standing in a scrapyard.

◇ Inside the box was her grandfather – the Doctor! He took off in the TARDIS with the teachers still on board, and they all had lots of adventures together.

◇ Susan was super-clever and knew loads about history, science and technology, but simple things like money confused her.

◇ She was sometimes easily frightened because of her sheltered life on Gallifrey, but she was always brave and loyal.

THE DOCTOR'S DIARY: REGENERATION

THE DALEK INVASION OF EARTH

We returned to Earth in 2164, only to find the Daleks had invaded and enslaved the entire planet. They said they were the Masters of Earth. Masters of Earth! Their plan was to mine the Earth's core, then pilot it around the galaxy. Have you ever heard such nonsense? Well, I soon put a stop to it. I found some brave humans, and we pitted our wits against the Daleks and defeated them. But, oh, my dear Susan. She decided to stay behind on Earth. I shall miss her so. But one day, I shall come back for her.

After an exhausting battle with the Cybermen at the South Pole, the Doctor felt his body start to change. He held it back for as long as he could, and even met the Twelfth Doctor before his time ran out.

MISSION 1: MATCH THE FLUID LINKS

I NEED TWO MATCHING FLUID LINKS TO GET THE TARDIS MOVING. FIND THE PAIR TO HELP ME BE ON MY WAY.

A B C

D E F

G H I

The SECOND DOCTOR

The Doctor's friends Ben and Polly were amazed when he turned into a completely new man!

THERE ARE SOME CORNERS OF THE UNIVERSE WHICH HAVE BRED THE MOST TERRIBLE THINGS. THINGS WHICH ACT AGAINST EVERYTHING WE BELIEVE IN. THEY MUST BE FOUGHT.

This new Doctor was friendlier and funnier, but anyone who thought he was just a clown was in trouble! He was as clever and sharp as ever, and would trick people to get his own way.

He enjoyed playing music on a recorder, but he also used the instrument to distract people – and sometimes even as a weapon! For the first time, the Doctor seemed to be telepathic – he could show people events from the past, and use his mind to take the fight right inside his enemies' heads.

He was much scruffier than before – he liked to wear big, baggy trousers and had wild, untidy hair.

ENEMY FILE: CYBERMEN

WHO WERE THEY?
Humans who had been enhanced with Cyber technology and had all of their emotions removed.

WHERE WERE THEY FROM?
Originally Mondas, but Cybermen had evolved all over the universe!

WHAT DID THEY WANT?
To upgrade everyone they could into Cybermen and increase their numbers.

WHAT HAPPENED WHEN THE DOCTOR MET THEM?
The Second Doctor wasn't the first to meet this species but he fought them often. Once, he had to deal with a whole tomb full of Cybermen when someone woke them up from hibernation! Another time, the Cybermen tried to take over the Earth by hypnotising everyone.

DANGER LEVEL: 95/100.

BEST FRIEND: *JAMIE McCRIMMON*

◇ Jamie was a Scottish piper who met the Doctor after fighting the English at the Battle of Culloden in 1746.

◇ He sneaked into the TARDIS to escape execution, and soon found himself fighting monsters, robots and evil geniuses instead of just soldiers!

◇ Being from the past, Jamie struggled to understand some of the strange things going on around him, but he was always keen to learn.

◇ Jamie sometimes disagreed with the Doctor's sneaky ways, especially when he put people's lives in danger.

◇ When the Doctor was captured by the Time Lords, Jamie was sent back to the Culloden battlefield. Nobody knows what happened to him next.

THE DOCTOR'S DIARY: REGENERATION

The Web of Fear

Oh, my word! What a day! We arrived in London only to find the Underground tunnels were full of webs. I know what you're thinking: giant spiders. Well, you're wrong. It was the Yeti. Yes, Abominable Snowmen! Jamie and I had fought them before, of course, but this time the Great Intelligence – the force that controls them – wanted to drain my brain. The cheek of it! I planned to turn the tables on it and drain its mind, but my silly friends rescued me and it got away. I suppose they meant well.

As punishment for stealing the TARDIS and interfering with history, the Doctor was forced by the Time Lords to change his appearance – and they also stranded him on Earth!

MISSION 2: MONSTER HUNT

S	D	M	C	T	B	G	O	I	R	E	S	L	E	V
M	R	A	Z	L	Q	H	N	X	T	L	Z	A	U	B
G	R	O	L	R	F	E	S	M	V	P	U	F	V	I
U	B	C	I	E	M	D	A	V	W	O	X	J	M	Z
S	Y	G	O	R	K	C	O	Y	W	E	I	V	Q	L
Q	B	S	E	E	R	S	R	G	M	P	F	A	O	O
I	P	B	Y	A	N	A	M	G	W	H	H	T	Z	L
T	Y	I	S	C	N	D	W	H	P	S	I	T	E	Y
C	H	T	L	G	O	W	W	E	A	I	Q	E	M	X
M	P	A	Y	M	G	D	R	M	C	F	U	A	Z	C
S	B	U	A	A	Z	Q	V	R	B	I	A	M	I	M
Y	H	B	G	H	R	P	H	B	T	N	R	O	S	X
A	M	V	F	K	P	X	Z	K	B	L	K	L	U	R
K	R	O	T	O	N	S	J	U	Q	U	S	L	M	D
Y	F	Q	I	J	C	A	T	X	N	U	G	D	W	Z

- DALEKS
- CYBERMEN
- YETI
- FISH PEOPLE
- ICE WARRIORS
- MACRA
- QUARKS
- KROTONS

The THIRD DOCTOR

This Doctor had to adjust to some big changes! The Time Lords ordered him to live on Earth, and even tampered with his TARDIS so it couldn't travel in time and space any more.

Then he had to get a job! He became a scientific adviser to UNIT, a special military organisation set up to deal with alien threats.

In this body, the Doctor was one cool guy! He dressed in snappy suits, wore frilly shirts and drove around in brilliant cars. He even did Venusian Aikido!

Even though he was handy in a fight, the Doctor still preferred to use words. He was an expert at negotiations.

The Doctor could sometimes seem a bit snooty, but he was still a free spirit who liked to do his own thing and hated being ordered around.

COURAGE ISN'T JUST A MATTER OF NOT BEING FRIGHTENED, YOU KNOW. IT'S BEING AFRAID AND DOING WHAT YOU HAVE TO DO ANYWAY.

ENEMY FILE: THE Master

WHO WAS HE?
The Master was another Time Lord. He grew up with the Doctor!

WHERE WAS HE FROM?
Gallifrey, the Doctor's home planet, in the constellation of Kasterborous.

WHAT DID HE WANT?
The Master got up to all kinds of crazy schemes, but most of the time he just wanted to annoy the Doctor!

WHAT HAPPENED WHEN THE DOCTOR MET HIM?
The Master arrived on Earth while the Third Doctor was in exile there, and teamed up with living plastic aliens to invade the planet. The Doctor stopped him, but he still kept turning up after that.

BEST FRIEND: JO GRANT

- Jo got a job at UNIT as the Doctor's laboratory assistant. He liked her right away and they ended up having lots of adventures together. She was great mates with the UNIT soldiers, especially the Doctor's boss, Brigadier Lethbridge-Stewart, and his troops Sergeant Benton and Captain Yates.
- Jo was devoted to the Doctor and hardly ever left his side – even though she often ended up in mortal danger!
- Eventually, Jo met Clifford Jones, a human scientist who was a lot like the Doctor. When she left UNIT to marry Clifford, the Doctor was heartbroken but knew she would be happy.
- Many years later, Jo met the Eleventh Doctor and had one more adventure with her old friend.

THE DOCTOR'S DIARY:

REGENERATION

The Green Death

Now, I've never trusted computers. What happened today only proves how right I am! The boss of a chemical company had his mind linked to a rogue computer that wanted to take over the human race. This company had been dumping deadly waste in a local mine, creating giant maggots and all sorts. I dealt with the megalomaniac machine and sorted out the pollution, of course. But my dear Jo met a decent young chap and she's gone off to marry him. I gave her a blue crystal from Metebelis III as a wedding present. Hope I don't need it again one day!

The Doctor stole the blue crystal he gave to Jo from the giant spiders of Metebelis III, and so the spiders went after the Doctor to get the crystal back. But when the Doctor went back to return it, he was flooded with radiation from all of the other crystals. He drifted through space for a long time before getting back to UNIT HQ, where he changed his face once again.

MISSION 3: *SWERVE THE SPIDERS*

The FOURTH DOCTOR

THERE'S NO POINT IN BEING GROWN-UP IF YOU CAN'T BE CHILDISH SOMETIMES.

After a few years spent mostly on Earth, this Doctor was keen to get back out and see the universe! He quit his job with UNIT, got in the TARDIS and set off.

The Time Lords repaired the Doctor's TARDIS, but they still sent him off on special missions for them – which he was never happy about. He even became their Lord President for a bit!

He got rid of all the previous Doctor's fancy clothes, and replaced them with a comfier style – big coats, curly hair, floppy hats and baggy trousers, plus his trademark super-long scarf.

His pockets were always full of useful bits and bobs, and he usually had a bag of jelly babies, which he would offer to people he met.

Sometimes it could be difficult to tell whose side the Doctor was on. He seemed to betray his own people when he let aliens invade Gallifrey, but it turned out to be a trick so he could defeat them.

BEST FRIEND: SARAH JANE SMITH

- Sarah Jane was a journalist who travelled with the Third and Fourth Doctors.
- They were best friends for years! The Doctor loved Sarah Jane's courage and warmth, but sometimes he had to watch out for her sharp tongue.
- Eventually, the Doctor had to leave her on Earth because he'd been summoned back to Gallifrey, where humans weren't allowed.
- The Doctor never forgot her, and sent her a K-9 of her very own.
- Much later, she bumped into the Tenth Doctor and suddenly found herself living her old life of adventure and danger again – and she loved it!

THE DOCTOR'S DIARY:

Pyramids of Mars

It's been a terribly thrilling couple of days, you know. Sarah and I arrived at an old house in 1911, where all sorts of things were going on. Sutekh, the last Osiran god, had been trapped inside a pyramid in Egypt by a signal from an identical pyramid on Mars. He was keen to get out – well, I don't blame him! – and he used some robot mummies to do it. I carelessly fell under his control and went to Mars myself. But, after I was freed, I used the TARDIS to shift the other end of the time tunnel Sutekh planned to escape through so that he would die before he ever reached the end, which I thought was rather clever.

ENEMY FILE: ZYGONS

WHO WERE THEY?
Shape-shifting aliens who could take on any form as long as they kept the person they were copying alive.

WHERE WERE THEY FROM?
Zygor, a planet that was destroyed in the Time War between the Time Lords and the Daleks.

WHAT DID THEY WANT?
A new home planet to replace the one they had lost.

WHAT HAPPENED WHEN THE DOCTOR MET THEM?
The Zygons' spaceship crash-landed in Loch Ness. They had brought a creature called a Skarasen with them and it was mistaken for the famous monster! Later, the Zygons tried to settle on Earth disguised as humans, but it proved hard to keep the peace.

DANGER LEVEL: 87/100.

REGENERATION

The Doctor faced his old enemy, the Master, at the top of a giant radio telescope. The Doctor fell off, but he didn't die. Instead, he regenerated and had a whole new face and body once more.

MISSION 4: SCARF STYLE

OH DEAR, MY SCARF SEEMS TO HAVE LOST ALL ITS COLOUR. THAT'LL NEVER DO. CAN YOU HELP ME RESTORE IT WITH YOUR COLOURING PENS AND PENCILS?

The FIFTH DOCTOR

This Doctor was a big change from the bold, booming one before. He was quieter and more thoughtful and sensitive than any of the other Doctors.

Although he seemed more serious than ever, this Doctor was actually very sarcastic and funny. His jokes were so clever that his enemies didn't realise he was making fun of them!

He wore a stick of celery in place of a flower on the lapel of his jacket. Everyone thought it was just the Doctor being the Doctor, but it was actually there to detect poisonous gas!

This Doctor liked to have a TARDIS full of pals – even though the ones he chose didn't always get on with each other.

THERE'S ALWAYS SOMETHING TO LOOK AT IF YOU OPEN YOUR EYES!

He was dressed in an old-fashioned cricket outfit, and was a great player too!

ENEMY FILE: THE SILURIANS

WHO WERE THEY?

Reptilian humanoids from a technologically advanced society.

WHERE WERE THEY FROM?

Earth. They ruled the planet at a time before humans had evolved, but then they went into hibernation.

WHAT DID THEY WANT?

To get their planet back! They weren't happy that it was ruled by 'the apes'.

WHAT HAPPENED WHEN THE DOCTOR MET THEM?

The Third Doctor tried to negotiate a peace treaty between the Silurians and humans, but his pals at UNIT ruined everything by blowing the Silurians up. Later, the Fifth Doctor met the survivors, who were still very angry. He tried once more to help humans and the Silurians get along with each other, but the two sides fought to the death.

DANGER LEVEL:

BEST FRIEND: TEGAN JOVANKA

◇ Tegan met the Doctor when she thought the TARDIS was a real police box and went inside looking for help.

◇ She was furious at being dragged along with the Doctor, and just wanted to get back to her cabin-crew job at Heathrow Airport.

◇ When he eventually got her back there, he left her behind, thinking that was what she wanted – but by then Tegan had changed her mind!

◇ Luckily, she bumped into him again a while later and asked to go with him once more.

◇ Sometimes the Doctor found Tegan hard to get along with, but underneath she was brave, kind and sensitive – just like the Doctor! It was these qualities that made her leave in the end, because she was upset by how many people had died on their adventures.

THE DOCTOR'S DIARY:

THE VISITATION

Well, I've had better days, I must say. It all started quietly enough. We landed in seventeenth-century England, only to find an android was pretending to be Death itself. A ship carrying three Terileptil convicts had crashed nearby, and it turned out they were responsible – so I soon sorted them out! Then, one of them hatched a plan to use rats to spread a plague and wipe out all life on Earth. We tracked the convicts to London and stopped them, but unfortunately a bit of a fire broke out. Well, more than a bit of a fire really. A Great Fire, you might even call it . . .

When the Doctor's new friend, Peri, caught a deadly illness called spectrox toxaemia, he had to get the milk of a queen bat to cure her. Unfortunately, he was infected too, but there was only enough milk for Peri, so the Doctor had to regenerate.

MISSION 5: *THE CAVES OF ANDROZANI*

The SIXTH DOCTOR

The Doctor quite often reacts against the personality of his last body, and he definitely did this time. Gone was the quiet, thoughtful man, and in his place came a loud, stubborn show-off!

Underneath this explosive exterior, though, the Doctor was still the Doctor – fighting for good and justice everywhere he went.

He replaced the beige cricket outfit with a bright coat in every possible colour and pattern, with trousers and a garish waistcoat to match, plus a cat badge on his lapel.

PLANETS COME AND GO. STARS PERISH. MATTER DISPERSES, COALESCES, FORMS INTO OTHER PATTERNS, OTHER WORLDS. NOTHING CAN BE ETERNAL.

Eventually, the Doctor was captured and put on trial by the Time Lords. He was threatened with execution if found guilty! But the trial fell apart when the prosecutor turned out to be an evil version of the Doctor from the future.

He was also fond of using long, complicated words to show how clever he was, and would often quote from obscure books and poems.

ENEMY FILE: THE SONTARANS

WHO WERE THEY?
A war-obsessed race of warrior clones.

WHERE WERE THEY FROM?
Sontar, but they travelled the universe in round spaceships.

WHAT DID THEY WANT?
War! They had been at war against their enemies, the Rutans, for a long time. Everything the Sontarans did was designed to defeat their foes.

WHAT HAPPENED WHEN THE DOCTOR MET THEM?
The Sixth Doctor clashed with the Ninth Sontaran Battle Fleet when they tried to gain time-travel technology to use in their endless war. Many other Doctors have fought them as well.

DANGER LEVEL: 88/100.

BEST FRIEND: PERI BROWN

- Peri was an American student on holiday with her family when she met the Fifth Doctor and was dragged into his latest adventure. She was in for a shock when her new friend changed his face not long after!
- The new Doctor was nothing like the man Peri knew, and she was frightened of his unpredictable moods. They argued a lot because his abrasive personality clashed with her laid-back attitude.
- Eventually, they grew to like each other again, but their happiness didn't last long, as Peri was killed when an alien slug transplanted his mind into her brain.
- The Doctor was relieved when he later found out that the Time Lords had tricked him and Peri was still alive – and was living as a warrior queen!

THE DOCTOR'S DIARY:

THE TRIAL OF A TIME LORD

It's an outrage! How could my own people, the Time Lords, set up such a wicked deception? I was plucked out of time and put on trial with evidence from my past, present and future served up to incriminate me. As if that wasn't enough, they also tampered with it to make it look like I was evil, that I put lives in danger with my meddling. My own people really are the most degenerate, warped civilisation in the entire universe. Ten million years of absolute power: that's what it takes to become really corrupt.

MISSION 6: FIND THE FOE

A O D T
L K N C R O
D H P S
I C P S K C L E

___ ___ ___   ___ ___ ___ ___

I HAVE A WAY WITH WORDS, BUT I'VE LOST TRACK OF THIS ONE. CROSS OUT THE REPEATED LETTERS, THEN USE THE LETTERS REMAINING TO SPELL THE NAME OF ONE OF MY ENEMIES.

When the Rani, a wicked Time Lord scientist, needed the Doctor to help with her latest experiment, she knew he wouldn't come willingly, so she ripped his TARDIS out of time. The Doctor was injured in the landing, which forced him to regenerate once more.

The SEVENTH DOCTOR

After a Doctor who had displayed every emotion on the surface, this next one was much more mysterious and secretive.

People who met the Doctor often thought he was a bit silly – he liked to fall over and play the spoons – but that was just a distraction from the secrets he held.

He even tried on a few of the other Doctors' old clothes before settling on his own look: a simple jacket and colourful patterned jumper, with a scarf and a special umbrella with a red question mark for a handle.

I CAN'T STAND BURNT TOAST. I LOATHE BUS STATIONS. TERRIBLE PLACES. FULL OF LOST LUGGAGE AND LOST SOULS.

His personality had shades of many other Doctors, such as the manipulative ways of the Second Doctor and the warm, caring nature of the Fifth Doctor.

The Doctor often encountered people who suggested there was more to him than met the eye, and that he was hiding secrets from the Old Times on Gallifrey – but we never found out what those secrets might have been.

ENEMY FILE: THE Destroyer

WHO WAS HE?
A terrifying blue demon with giant horns.

WHERE WAS HE FROM?
Another dimension.

WHAT DID HE WANT?
To devour the Earth! They didn't call him the Eater of Worlds for nothing, you know.

WHAT HAPPENED WHEN THE DOCTOR MET HIM?
A witch called Morgaine thought she could control the Destroyer by binding him in silver, but he was too strong and escaped. After being pursued by the Doctor and the Brigadier, he was eventually shot with silver bullets – all before he could do any world-devouring!

62/100.

BEST FRIEND: ACE

◇ The Doctor met sixteen-year-old Ace in an alien supermarket called Iceworld. She had ended up there because of a time storm she'd accidentally whipped up in her bedroom on Earth. Ace was an expert in blowing things up, and the Doctor liked her cheeky and brave nature so he invited her to travel with him.

◇ She nicknamed him 'Professor' and they had lots of great adventures.

◇ As time went on, however, she realised that she hadn't ended up on Iceworld by accident at all; the Doctor had been involved all along.

◇ Ace wasn't happy that the Doctor had been manipulating her life, but they made up in the end and continued their travels for many years.

THE DOCTOR'S DIARY: REGENERATION

The Happiness Patrol

Always be suspicious of someone who says they're happy all the time. I met a woman tonight called Helen A. She was in charge of Terra Alpha, and seemed to think that happiness would prevail if only everyone wore a fake smile all the time. She even had a man made of sweets to execute people who weren't cheery enough, which definitely didn't make me happy. I warned her to mend her ways or I'd mend them for her, but in the end she brought about her own downfall. She lost her beloved pet, and learned then that happiness is nothing unless it exists side by side with sadness.

In San Francisco, the Doctor was accidentally shot. A local surgeon tried to operate on him without realising he wasn't human and he seemed to have died. However, when the anaesthetic wore off several hours later, he was finally able to regenerate.

MISSION 7: THE RUNES OF FENRIC

I BATTLED THE ANCIENT POWER OF FENRIC. HELP ME DECODE THE ANCIENT CURSE USING THE SPECIAL KEY.

A B C D E F G H I J K L M

N O P Q R S T U V W X Y Z

___ ______ __ ______

_____ ______ ___

_____ _______.

The EIGHTH DOCTOR

In need of new clothes, the Doctor nicked a costume someone at the hospital was planning to wear to a New Year's party. It looked a lot like the kind of thing his earliest faces might have worn – he had a waistcoat, long coat, high boots and a neck tie.

Most people would avoid the person who nearly killed them accidentally, but not the Doctor! He immediately became friends with Dr Grace Holloway, the surgeon who caused his regeneration.

This Doctor was a charming adventurer who loved life, even as the universe became more and more violent and angry.

While he was recovering, the Master turned up – as a large snake! He soon took over a human body, though, and was back in business.

FOUR MINUTES? THAT'S AGES! WHAT IF I GET BORED, OR NEED A TELEVISION, A COUPLE OF BOOKS? ANYONE FOR CHESS? BRING ME KNITTING.

When the Time War raged, the Doctor tried to stay out of it, but eventually realised he had to join the fight.

REGENERATION

The Doctor was on board a ship that crash-landed on Karn. He died in the crash, but the Sisterhood of Karn brought him back to life. He knew he had to become a warrior to save the universe from the Time War, so he took the Elixir of Life to kick-start his regeneration.

MISSION 8: KARN CHALLENGE

TIME IS COLLAPSING! HELP ME FIND THE FIVE DIFFERENCES BETWEEN THESE TWO SCENES, SO THE SISTERHOOD OF KARN CAN GET THINGS BACK TO NORMAL.

THE WARRIOR

DOCTOR NO MORE.

The Doctor had changed like never before. He was now a warrior and refused to take his old name.

The Time War between the Daleks and the Time Lords had begun, so he became the man he needed to be: someone who would do whatever it took to end the war.

When he first changed, he was young and strong. But the war went on and on, and was still raging when he eventually became an old man.

He then realised the war would never end unless someone took drastic action by killing all the Daleks and all the Time Lords.

That was until he met the Tenth and Eleventh Doctors, and they came up with a daring plan to end the war without any more death. He then felt proud enough to take on the name of the Doctor again – even though he would never remember his last adventure.

REGENERATION

After living through the hell of the Time War, the Doctor regenerated due to old age for the very first time.

HIDDEN MISSION: TIME WAR TEST

REMOON

___ ___   ___ ___ ___ ___

THE MOMENT HAS JUMBLED UP MY MESSAGE TO THE DALEKS. CAN YOU UNSCRAMBLE THE LETTERS TO REVEAL THE TRUTH?

The ELEVENTH DOCTOR

Up to this point, the Doctor had managed to slip under the radar. His best enemies knew him well, but he could turn up pretty much anywhere in the universe and no one would know who he was. All that was about to change.

This new Doctor might have looked more youthful than ever, but in that fresh face hid old, weary eyes. He could sometimes be almost as grumpy as his very first face, but also managed to have a childish delight for life.

He travelled mainly with Amy and Rory, a married couple who turned out to be the parents of the Doctor's old friend River Song.

WE'RE ALL STORIES IN THE END. JUST MAKE IT A GOOD ONE, EH? COS IT WAS, YOU KNOW. IT WAS THE BEST. A DAFT OLD MAN WHO STOLE A MAGIC BOX AND RAN AWAY.

This Doctor's clothes weren't quite as cool as the previous Doctor's. His first look was a tweed jacket and bow tie, which he would often accessorise with an ill-matched hat (he especially loved his red fez).

When the Doctor lost Amy and Rory, he became sadder and more pensive, and his clothes changed to reflect this.

This Doctor lived for many thousands of years, and for a while it looked like he might be the last Doctor ever . . .

ENEMY FILE: WEEPING ANGELS

WHO WERE THEY?
Quantum-locked aliens disguised as statues.

WHERE WERE THEY FROM?
Nobody knows – they were almost as old as the universe!

WHAT DID THEY WANT?
To send people into the past, then live off the potential energy of the life their victims would have lived in the present.

WHAT HAPPENED WHEN THE DOCTOR MET THEM?
He encountered them more than once, but the worst time was when an angel sent Amy and Rory back to 1938 – forever. The Doctor was so angry he trapped all the angels in a crack in time.

DANGER LEVEL: 96/100.

BEST FRIEND: AMY POND

◇ When Amelia Pond was seven years old, she was kept awake by a terrible crack in her bedroom wall.

◇ Then, one day, a strange man crashed in to her garden – the Doctor! He promised to come back for her in five minutes, but he took twelve years.

◇ When Amy finally got on board the TARDIS, it was the start of the trip of a lifetime! She was always up for an adventure, and kept the Doctor on his toes with her sense of humour and determined ways.

◇ She eventually got married, but unlike Jo Grant she brought her husband along on the TARDIS with her! She and Rory even had a baby, called Melody Pond, who grew up to be River Song and was part-Time Lord.

THE DOCTOR'S DIARY: REGENERATION

THE PANDORICA OPENS

Okay, buckle up, because this is a complicated one. Amy Pond got shot by her boyfriend, Rory, except Rory was an Auton, except now he's human again, but that bit comes later. I got Rory to put Amy in the Pandorica and guard it for thousands of years, which was fine as he was made of plastic at the time. Then Amy's younger self opened it up, and the box used the sample of her DNA to bring the adult Amy back to life. Then I got in it again, but that's another story.

The Doctor vowed to protect a planet that was in danger from an alliance of his worst enemies. He stayed there until he was absolutely ancient and was convinced he would die, as he'd run out of regenerations. Luckily, the Time Lords sent him a whole new cycle through a crack in time.

MISSION 11: DON'T BLINK

The TWELFTH DOCTOR

Over time, the Doctor started to cheer up a bit, especially when he was reunited with his old friend River Song.

This Doctor started out as a snappy dresser, wearing a smart coat with a red lining, a white shirt and long black boots. He kept the coat, but the stuff he wore underneath became much scruffier over time, and he soon started dressing like a rock star! His hair (and his eyebrows!) had also grown impressively by the time he regenerated.

The Twelfth Doctor was a much more stern and fiery character than any of the others. He could be rude, ruthless and cold, but the Doctor's usual character was always there under the surface.

When he travelled with Clara Oswald, he worried that he was no longer a good man like all the other Doctors had been. As he and Clara became better friends, he worried about this much less.

NEVER BE CRUEL, NEVER BE COWARDLY, AND NEVER, EVER EAT PEARS! REMEMBER, HATE IS ALWAYS FOOLISH, AND LOVE IS ALWAYS WISE. ALWAYS TRY TO BE NICE, BUT NEVER FAIL TO BE KIND.

He was consumed for a long time with a strong desire to find his home planet, Gallifrey. However, when he finally tracked it down, the first thing he wanted to do was run away again!

ENEMY FILE: MISSY

WHO WAS SHE?
The Doctor's old enemy the Master, now regenerated into female form.

WHERE WAS SHE FROM?
Gallifrey.

WHAT DID SHE WANT?
At first, Missy just wanted to be evil, as usual. But, after spending years locked in a vault, she changed her ways and started to regret all the people she'd killed.

WHAT HAPPENED WHEN THE DOCTOR MET HER?
Just when it looked like Missy had joined the Doctor's side, an old version of the Master appeared and led her astray once again. However, Missy switched sides once more to help the Doctor during his final battle with the Cybermen, which resulted in her and the Master stabbing each other in the back. But are they really gone for good?

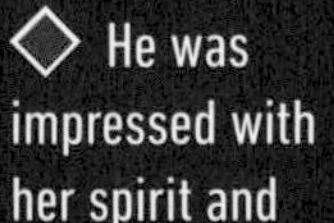

BEST FRIEND: BILL POTTS

◇ The Doctor got a job at a university, and Bill, who worked in the canteen, was sneaking in to his lectures.

◇ He was impressed with her spirit and determination, and offered to be her personal tutor. Bill had no idea what that meant when she agreed to it!

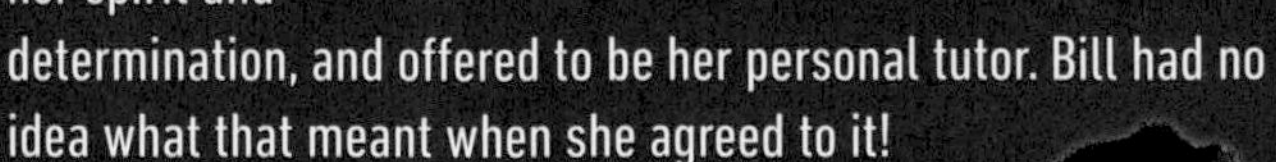

◇ She was soon whizzing through all of time and space with him, marvelling at the amazing things she saw.

◇ Poor Bill was turned into a Cyberman and her body died, but her girlfriend Heather appeared to rescue her spirit and they're now exploring the universe together!

THE DOCTOR'S DIARY:

WORLD ENOUGH AND TIME

I've had dark days before, but never anything like this. For some reason, I thought it would be a good idea to test Missy – see if she really was reformed. But she messed it up, and Bill ended up in a different time zone. I couldn't get to her in time, and she fell into the wrong hands: specifically the Master's, before he became Missy. Bill waited for me, but I was too slow and it was too late. She became a Cyberman.

REGENERATION

After an almighty battle with the Mondasian Cybermen, the Doctor was electrocuted, shot and blown up, and lay close to death. He tried to stop the regeneration process, but eventually accepted his fate and changed once more.

MISSION 12: THE NAME OF THE DOCTOR

USE THIS GUIDE TO GALLIFREYAN LETTERS TO TRANSLATE MY NAME INTO MY OWN LANGUAGE – THEN SEE IF YOU CAN DO YOURS!

 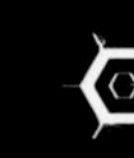  

A B C D

E F G H

I J K L

M N O P

Q R S T

U V W X

Y Z

The Doctor

Your name

The DOCTOR FALLS

I'M BILL POTTS,
AND I'M DEAD.

Don't worry, though, it's not as bad as it sounds. Cos I say I'm dead, but in some ways I'm more alive than ever, but I'll get to that in a minute.

It all started so well. I had a job dishing up chips in the Uni canteen, but then I met the Doctor and he said he'd be my tutor. I didn't realise exactly what that meant at first. That my life would never be the same again.

We went everywhere together, had such amazing adventures. And then I died for the first time. Boom. Massive hole in my chest. Nobody could survive that. But I did. I got separated from the Doctor and they turned me into this thing. They said I was a Cyberman, but inside I still felt like Bill.

I thought I'd never see the Doctor again, but I did – sort of. My memories had been collected up into a sort of box that looked and acted just like me, and we had one more adventure. We even met this old guy who reckoned he was the Doctor too.

But the Doctor was only ever holding off the end, and when we said goodbye again, I knew I would never see him again.

Did I say I was dead? Well, I was. Heather brought me back - the girl who was was given amazing powers by a crashed alien ship. We left together to explore the stars. Maybe I'll see you again, out there?

WHERE'S THE DOCTOR? PART 2

I KNOW! IF I WAS YOU I'D WANT TO EAT ME TOO. BUT CAN'T WE JUST TALK ABOUT THIS?

NOT SO FAST, LIZARD. I WANT THE PLEASURE OF KILLING THIS ONE MYSELF.
RUDE!
HOLD ON. THAT'S A TRANSMAT BEACON. YOU SHOULDN'T HAVE THAT.

PROBABLY NOT. BUT, SINCE I DO, WHY DON'T THE TWO OF US TAKE A SHORT TRIP?

NO THANKS. I'M QUITE HAPPY HERE.
ANYWAY, YOU'VE GOT MORE TO WORRY ABOUT THAN ME.

NOOOOOOOOOO!
ACTUALLY, YES. SORRY!

I'VE SEEN THAT WOMAN BEFORE. LOTS OF BEFORES IN FACT.
GRAHAM!

YOU HOLLERED, BOSS?
WE'VE GOT A PROBLEM.

I NEED TO FOLLOW THAT LIZARD!
PUBLIC CALL

DOC, ONLY YOU COULD STIR UP A GIANT ALIEN LIZARD ON CORONATION DAY.
BRILLIANT, ISN'T SHE?
HAVE YOU GOT A SIGNAL?
YUP. STRONG! THE TARDIS CAN PULL US THROUGH.

I'LL LAND DISCREETLY - GIVE US TIME TO COME UP WITH A PLAN.

MEANWHILE . . .
OH, HERE SHE IS. THE MOST FEARED ASSASSIN IN THE TWELVE QUADRANTS.
DO YOU MIND? I'M REALLY NOT IN THE MOOD.

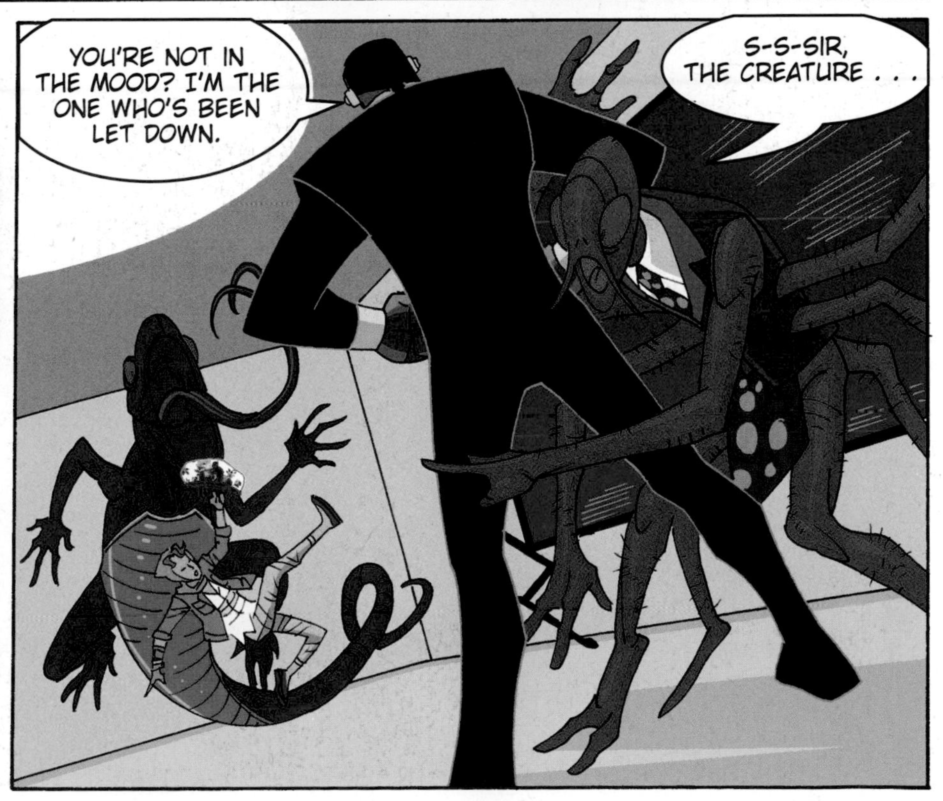
YOU'RE NOT IN THE MOOD? I'M THE ONE WHO'S BEEN LET DOWN.
S-S-SIR, THE CREATURE . . .

ONE SIMPLE JOB. KILL THE DOCTOR.
DOES SHE LOOK DEAD TO YOU?
THERE WERE TOO MANY TRACES! SHE WAS IN A DOZEN PLACES AT ONCE.

THERE'S ONLY ONE PLACE SHE'S HEADING NOW. HERE!
YOU'VE BROUGHT THE DOCTOR TO MY DOOR.

FORTUNATELY, WE KNOW SHE'S COMING. SHE'S LOST THE ELEMENT OF --
VWORP!
VWORP!
POLICE PUBLIC CALL BOX
CRASHH!

SURPRISE!
AS I SAID. DISCREET.
POLICE
OX

I'M THE DOCTOR, AND THIS IS MY GANG.
AND YOU ARE?
POLICE
POLICE
BOX

EVA DE VILLE. AND THAT HEAP OF JUNK WAS THE CEO, WHO HIRED ME TO KILL YOU.
WELL, YOU'RE A RUBBISH ASSASSIN. ALL YOU'VE DONE TODAY IS SAVE ME.
THIRTEEN TIMES AND COUNTING.

NO! YOU WERE . . . ALL OF THEM?
WELL, STRICTLY SPEAKING, ALL OF THEM WERE ME. BUT YES.
ANYWAY, YOUR ROBOT PAL'S DECOMMISSIONED, SO LET'S CALL THIS WHOLE HIT OFF, EH?

STRICTLY SPEAKING, SHE WAS HIRED BY ME. HE WAS THE CEO . . .
BUT I'M THE CHAIRMAN.

OHHHHH. INSECTOID GANGSTER IN THIS PART OF THE GALAXY? YOU MUST BE WITH THE PHASMATODEA CARTEL . . .
FOR NOW, UNTIL I SHUT IT DOWN.
CHARMED, I'M SURE.
NOW, TIME TO DIE.

CHAIRMAN, YOU'RE IN DANGER! PUT THE GUN DOWN. YOU FORGOT ABOUT THE --
YOU MUST THINK I HATCHED YESTERDAY, DOCTOR. IT'S NOT ME WHO'S IN --

DANGERRRRRRRR!
CRUNCH!
GULP!
SLURRRRP!

EVERYONE KNOWS LIZARDS CAN'T RESIST INSECTS.
YOU DID TRY TO WARN HIM.

WELL, I THINK I'LL BE GOING NOW.
NO CHANCE! THE ONLY PLACE YOU'RE GOING IS JAIL.

RIGHT AFTER WE GET OLD LIZARD-FEATURES BACK HOME.
BIT OF RESPECT, RYAN. THIS ISN'T JUST ANY GIANT LIZARD. SHE'S THE QUEEN.

OR, AS I'VE ALWAYS CALLED HER . . .
LIZ!
HISSSSSS!

The THIRTEENTH DOCTOR

I'M THE DOCTOR. SORTING OUT FAIR PLAY THROUGHOUT THE UNIVERSE.

THE BASICS

FULL NAME: **The Doctor**

AGE: **Mind your own business!**

FROM: **Gallifrey, constellation of Kasterborous**

OCCUPATION: **Being the Doctor**

TARDIS Personality Test

FAIR SQUAD DIRECT EXCITEMENT HONEST JUSTICE THIRTEENTH RIGHT SILLY TEAM TARDIS HEROIC WONDER ADVENTURE BRAVE SONIC LOVING FUNNY DANGER FRIENDS

The new Doctor is a real ball of energy. She was fizzing with it from the moment we met her – literally!

She's been wide-eyed and excitable from the moment of her regeneration, and is ready to rediscover all the wonders of time and space through new eyes.

She's confident and fearless in the face of danger. She's definitely not scared of standing up for her friends when they are in peril.

The universe is a dangerous place, but this Doctor is dedicated to bringing justice wherever she goes.

This Doctor is sensitive and caring, but don't mistake that for weakness. She can turn angry in a flash when confronted with cruelty or injustice.

Most of all, this Doctor just wants to help.

'When people need help, I never refuse!'

FRIENDS AND FAMILY

- The Doctor's team are her closest friends, and she trusts them more than anyone else.
- She also helps them to be the very best they can be, and isn't shy about telling them how amazing she thinks they are.
- That doesn't mean they can get away with anything, though! She wants her friends to think before they act.
- She encourages the team to stick together when necessary, but also helps them to strike out on their own.
- The friendship goes two ways, and the Doctor has plenty to learn from her mates as well.

THE DOCTOR AND . . .

RYAN

◇ The Doctor knows Ryan is capable of achieving great things – even if he doesn't always believe it himself!

◇ She gives him lots of praise, but also pulls him up when he leaps into action without thinking first.

YAZ

◇ She's the Doctor's right-hand woman, helping her to lead the gang on their adventures.

◇ The Doctor sees a lot of herself in Yaz, and likes her ambitious, confident nature.

GRAHAM

◇ There's a huge amount of mutual respect between the Doctor and Graham. Sometimes he even calls her 'Boss'!

◇ However, he doesn't always understand her instinct to jump head first into danger.

WhosApp

GRAHAM
Doc, just checking. You do know where the TARDIS is, right?

THE DOCTOR
Yeah, of course. Well, roughly.

GRAHAM
I can tell you exactly where it is. It's in my back garden. And It's upside down.

THE DOCTOR
Wow, that's SO interesting! But I can't really chat at the moment. I'm . . . a bit busy.

RYAN
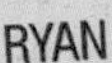  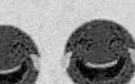
You're upside down too, aren't you? I thought I was bad!

THE DOCTOR
Nooooo! Absolutely not. One hundred per cent the right way up. I've TOTALLY got the hang of landing the TARDIS now.

YAZ

Just hang on, Doctor. We're on our way.

THE DOCTOR
If I could hang on, I wouldn't be upside down. Which of course I'm not.

The New TARDIS!

Sometimes when the Doctor regenerates, the TARDIS goes through some changes too! For example:

◇ The Thirteenth Doctor's TARDIS is a different shade of blue than the Twelfth Doctor's.

◇ The sign on the door is now black with white lettering.

◇ The door handle is now below the keyhole instead of above it.

◇ The light on top is a different shape.

The ADVENTURE Begins

INCIDENT REPORT

Reporting Officer: PC YASMIN KHAN

Case No.: CLASSIFIED

Location: CLASSIFIED

Date: CLASSIFIED

Other officers deployed: SERGEANT RAMESH SUNDER

RECOUNT:

I DON'T EVEN KNOW WHY I'M FILING THIS REPORT. THE DOCTOR TOLD ME NOT TO BOTHER, BUT I HAVE TO. IT ALL STARTED WHEN I GOT A CALL-OUT TO THE SIGHTING OF A STRANGE OBJECT. IT HAD BEEN REPORTED BY A MALE, AGE NINETEEN, CALLED RYAN SINCLAIR. NO, THAT SOUNDS WRONG. I CAN'T JUST CALL HIM 'A MALE' – HE'S MY FRIEND RYAN. ANYWAY, HE'D SIGHTED A BULB-SHAPED OBJECT THAT WAS THROBBING AND VIBRATING, AND FIZZED TO THE TOUCH.

RYAN HAD GOT A CALL FROM HIS GRANDPARENTS, GRAHAM AND GRACE, TO SAY THEIR TRAIN HAD STOPPED AND WEIRD STUFF WAS HAPPENING. THEY SAID SOMEONE HAD FALLEN THROUGH THE ROOF. AND THAT'S HOW WE ALL MET THE DOCTOR. SHE SAID SHE WAS AN ALIEN WHO ONLY WANTED TO HELP, AND I BELIEVED HER.

TURNS OUT SHE WASN'T THE ONLY ALIEN AROUND. THERE WAS ALSO A MASSIVE TENTACLE THING AND A HUGE GUY IN SOME SERIOUS ARMOUR. THE DOCTOR THOUGHT THEY HAD COME TO EARTH FOR A SCRAP, BUT THE TRUTH WAS EVEN WORSE.

THE ARMOURED GUY – I THINK HE SAID HIS NAME WAS TIM SHAW, BUT HE DIDN'T LOOK MUCH LIKE A TIM TO ME – CAME HERE ON A MISSION. HE WAS A STENZA WARRIOR, AND APPARENTLY THEIR THING IS HUNTING ONE SINGLE PERSON ON A PLANET AND CLAIMING THEM FOR A TROPHY. HE HAD A FACE STUDDED WITH THE TEETH OF THE PEOPLE HE'D HUNTED.

THE DOCTOR WOULDN'T STAND FOR THAT, AND SHE DEFEATED 'TIM'. I CAN'T SAY EXACTLY HOW – IT'S TOP SECRET – BUT I CAN TELL YOU THAT SHE DID A PRETTY COOL JUMP FROM ONE CRANE TO ANOTHER. SHE WAS AMAZING. WE ALL WERE.

EVIDENCE REPORT

THE DOCTOR MADE THIS SCANNER THING. A SONIC SCREWDRIVER, SHE CALLED IT – NEVER SAW HER SCREW ANYTHING IN WITH IT, THOUGH.
SHE TOOK A LOAD OF CIRCUITS, GROUND DOWN SOME LED LIGHTS, CHISELLED SOME ALIEN TECH OFF THE STENZA'S BULB THING, MELTED DOWN A LOAD OF CUTLERY, THEN WELDED IT ALL TOGETHER AND, FOR SOME REASON, SPRAYED IT WITH FIRE-EXTINGUISHER FOAM. SHE MADE IT LOOK SO EASY, AS THOUGH SHE DID THAT SORT OF THING EVERY DAY.

Meet RYAN

THE BASICS

FULL NAME: Ryan Sinclair

AGE: 19

FROM: Sheffield, United Kingdom, Earth

OCCUPATION: Trainee Mechanic

TARDIS Personality Test

TECH
SWEET CARING
GRANDSON
ENERGETIC GROUNDED
TRUSTING VLOGGER MECHANIC
CURIOUS IMPULSIVE INSTINCTIVE
NVQ
QUICK
DYSPRAXIC
BRAINS OVER BULLETS

IT'S LIKE I'M SCARED OF WHAT'S ABOUT TO HAPPEN, BUT ALSO I DON'T WANT IT TO STOP!

Ryan's mum died when he was small, so he's been brought up by his nan, Grace.

He's studying to be a mechanic – he's very handy with machines and tech! He also has a job in a warehouse, which he hates, but it's only until he finishes his studies.

Sometimes Ryan gets frustrated because of his dyspraxia, a condition that can cause him problems with co-ordination and moving around.

He's very instinctive, and can make rash choices when put on the spot – something the Doctor tries to teach him not to do!

When he's not working or studying, he's into gaming and also loves working on his vlogs.

FRIENDS AND FAMILY

- Ryan's always been close to his nan, Grace, and calls her the greatest woman he's ever met.
- She can tell exactly how he'll react when he faces something challenging, even before he knows himself!
- They've been a team for so long that he struggles to cope when she's not around.

WhosApp

RYAN
Doctor! If you saw something really weird and glowy at the bus stop, what would you do?

THE DOCTOR
Ryan, please don't touch the weird glowy thing.

RYAN
Okay, so, hypothetically, if you had given it a tiny kick, and now your foot was glowing too, what would you do then? Hypothetically.

THE DOCTOR
Did you kick it, Ryan?

RYAN
No no no no. This is all hypothetical. But say I didn't mean to. Say I just kind of tripped over it.

THE DOCTOR
Hypothetically?

RYAN
Yeah, hypothetically.

THE DOCTOR
Well, totally hypothetically, I'd tell you to stick your foot in a bucket of water as fast as you can and pray it doesn't fall off before I get there.

RYAN
Cool.

RYAN AND . . .

THE DOCTOR

- At first, Ryan's a bit nervous – scared, even – of the Doctor, but his desire for adventure and curiosity mean he finds life with her irresistible!
- The Doctor really boosts his confidence. She's impressed with his tech skills, logic and quick thinking. She knows he's capable of anything he puts his mind to, and always encourages him to do his best.

YAZ

- Ryan went to primary school with Yaz, but hasn't seen her since. They're happy to meet again, though!
- They tease each other all the time. He's always happy to get a compliment from her, as it doesn't happen often.

GRAHAM

- Ryan didn't always get on with Graham after he and Grace got married, but he could see that Graham made her very happy.
- But perhaps some time – and some adventures! – together is just what they need to learn more about each other and grow closer.

Into the TARDIS

Hi, guys. Ryan here.

Actually, this one's just for me – I can't upload this to the internet. But I needed to talk about what's been happening.

VIDEO DIARY

00.13

I've got this friend, **the Doctor**, and she's **like nobody you've ever known before.** Not long after I first met her, she tried to track down her spaceship, **the TARDIS.** She said she had a lock on it with her **sonic screwdriver,** and she tried to pull us through to where it was – but there was nothing there. **Just space. Not great.**

Anyway, we got rescued by these two ships. Graham and I went on the *Orme* with Angstrom, but the Doctor and Yaz went on the *Cerberus* with another guy. The two pilots were in this crazy competition called **the Rally of the Twelve Galaxies.** Four thousand ships had entered, but only these two had survived. The winner would get some **rich guy's fortune,** while the loser would be **stranded on a planet called Desolation. Talk about all or nothing!**

To win this rally you had to be the **first to the Ghost Monument, a blue box** that made this wheezing, groaning sound but kept vanishing and reappearing. **Turns out the Ghost Monument was actually the Doctor's spaceship.**

Getting to it was hard work, man! We crossed mist swamps, got shot at by Sniperbots and almost strangled by vicious creatures called Whispers, but we made it and the Doctor got her spaceship back.

That was just the start of it all, though. The really amazing stuff was on the other side of those blue doors: **the TARDIS!**

TARDIS Q&A

I'VE ANSWERED ALL YOUR QUESTIONS ABOUT THE TARDIS, EVEN THOUGH YOU HAVEN'T ASKED THEM YET. THAT SOMETIMES HAPPENS WITH TIME TRAVEL.

TARDIS stands for Time and Relative Dimension in Space.

It's bigger on the inside than the outside. How? Well, imagine a little box, then a big box so far away it fits inside the little box that is also in the same place as the little box. Simple!

It's supposed to be able to ***change shape*** to match wherever it lands, but it ***got stuck as a police box*** and I decided I liked it that way.

I didn't build it. ***I stole it!*** Or it stole me. Depends who you're asking.

When I regenerated, it ***blew up***. It took itself off for a bit of a rest, but the planet it was on fell out of orbit and ***I lost it*** . . . until I ***found it again.***

While it was gone, it ***redecorated itself.*** I love it! Especially the glowy orange bit in the middle. It's brilliant!

Look at that console! Gorgeous, isn't it. It's got so many bits. I might add even more bits – see what happens. ***What could possibly go wrong?***

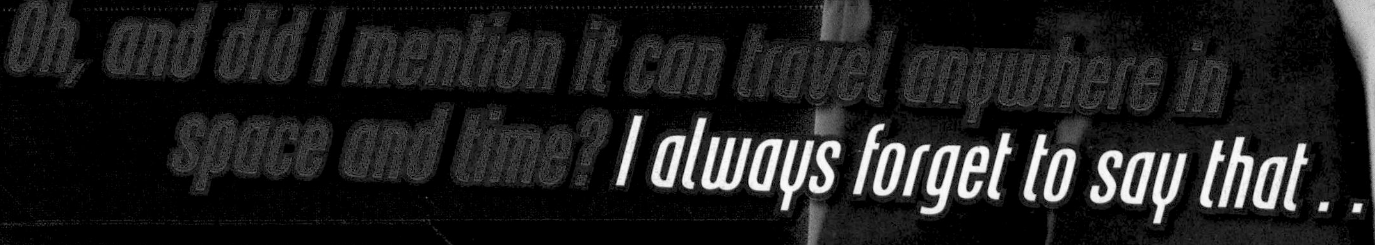

Meet YASMIN

THE BASICS

FULL NAME: **Yasmin (Yaz) Khan**

AGE: **19**

FROM: **Sheffield, United Kingdom, Earth**

OCCUPATION: **Police officer**

D'YOU THINK THIS MAKES ME THE FIRST YORKSHIREWOMAN IN SPACE?

Yaz is up for any challenge the world throws her way – the bigger the better, in fact! She loves new experiences and the thrill of adventure.

Thanks to her police training, she's really observant and always notices when something suspicious is going on.

She's tough and fearless, brilliant at calming down explosive situations, and a natural leader who comes up with plans in a flash.

Whenever there's danger, she's right by the Doctor's side, leading the gang. Yaz is amazing on her own, but she's unbeatable when paired up with the Doctor!

She doesn't always have all the answers – not in her job as a trainee PC or in her life with the Doctor – and she can get frustrated when her plans aren't enough to save everyone.

TARDIS Personality Test

POLICE BOX

TOUGH KIND POLICE
PERCEPTIVE
FEARLESS CONFIDENT HEADSTRONG
HELPER EXCITABLE OBSERVANT LOGICAL DYNAMIC
DECISIVE
LEADER LEARNING PROTECTIVE
CALM ENERGY
DIPLOMATIC
HOW CAN I HELP?

FRIENDS AND FAMILY

- Yaz is from a big, close-knit family – there's always something going on and someone who needs looking after!
- She's training to be a police officer with Hallamshire Police, and loves her job because she can help people every day.
- While she loves her family, she wants more out of life and to get out of her comfort zone!

WhosApp

YAZ
Doctor, can I ask you a personal question?

THE DOCTOR
Course you can! I might even answer it, seeing as it's you.

YAZ
So, you know how you told me you used to be a white-haired Scotsman?

THE DOCTOR
Yeah! That was brilliant. I loved that guy. Even if he didn't let me eat pears.

YAZ
Well, if you used to be him, have you ever been anyone else?

THE DOCTOR
I've been loads of people. They're all still in my head somewhere.

YAZ
Doesn't it get noisy in there?

THE DOCTOR
Sometimes. I listen when I want to, but I know my own mind. And I'm the oldest, so I know better than all of them put together.

YAZ
I get you. At least, I think I do.

YAZ AND . . .

THE DOCTOR

- Yaz and the Doctor are a dynamic duo. They each have a duty to protect those in need, so they get on well from the start.
- Yaz sometimes takes too much on and gets out of her depth, but the Doctor is always happy to let her lead the gang on their adventures.

RYAN

- Yaz has lots of respect for Ryan but that doesn't mean she doesn't enjoy winding him up sometimes!
- They complement each other well – she knows about history, while he's stronger on gadgets and tech.

GRAHAM

- Yaz isn't part of Graham's family like Ryan is, but they still have a great friendship.
- Graham is naturally more cautious than Yaz, and worries about her when she puts herself in danger.

TARDIS TWINS

The TARDIS has been caught in a fractal replicator, and now the Doctor is left with loads of tiny TARDISes! Only two of them are exactly the same. Match them up and the TARDIS will go back to normal.

A

B

C

D

E

THE TARDIS HAS GONE A BIT WEIRD. CAN YOU HELP ME?

F

G

H

I

TIME TWISTED

Can you spot the 8 differences between these two parallel worlds?

Meet GRAHAM

THE BASICS

FULL NAME: **Graham O'Brien**

AGE: **Late fifties**

FROM: **Sheffield, United Kingdom, Earth**

OCCUPATION: **Former bus driver**

TARDIS Personality Test

SOLID WISE BRAVE
DEPENDABLE
CHARMING
STRONG
FAMILY
PRACTICAL CHEEKY FUNNY FRIENDLY
WORRIER
WEST HAM
SECOND CHANCE AT LIFE

THERE'S NO SUCH THING AS ALIENS. AND, EVEN IF THERE WAS, THEY'RE NOT GONNA BE ON A TRAIN IN SHEFFIELD!

Graham's from Essex but moved to Sheffield to be with his wife, Grace. He's a bit of a joker and is always making gags.

After surviving a tough illness, he's making the most of every second! He's so excited to have met the Doctor and to have the chance to see the universe.

He's solid and dependable, and although he'd never run from danger he doesn't understand why everyone isn't as scared as he is of the creatures and worlds they encounter!

Graham's a great guy to travel with. He can make friends with anyone, even in a tricky period of history or on an alien planet!

He tries to see the best in everyone, but this means that sometimes he can be blind to others' faults.

FRIENDS AND FAMILY

Graham was nursed by Grace when he was ill. They fell in love and got married, and were making the most of life together when the Doctor crashed into their lives.

Graham is more practical than outgoing Grace, and he finds himself a bit lost travelling the universe without her.

To get around this, he often asks himself, 'What would Grace do?' when he has a problem.

Graham wants to be a good grandad to Ryan, but he has to work hard to gain Ryan's trust.

WhosApp

GRAHAM
Boss, can you take me somewhere in the TARDIS?

THE DOCTOR
I can take you somewhere. Might not be where you want to go, though.

GRAHAM
Well, I was thinking Wembley Stadium. Tenth of May 1980.

THE DOCTOR
Is this a West Ham thing?

GRAHAM
Not just any thing! That's the day we spanked the Gunners 1–0 and lifted the FA Cup.

THE DOCTOR
Hold on. 1980? Were you there?

GRAHAM
Well, yeah . . . but it was such a good game that I wanna see it again.

THE DOCTOR
No can do. Have you never heard of Blinovitch?

GRAHAM
I think so. Midfielder, played for Red Star Belgrade?

THE DOCTOR
Not quite. Physicist, discovered that really bad stuff happens if past and future versions of the same person meet.

GRAHAM
Oh, right. Not ideal. What about the day before, then?

THE DOCTOR
Was there a match then too?

GRAHAM
No, but I could put a few quid on the Hammers to win . . .

GRAHAM AND . . .

THE DOCTOR

◆ Graham and the Doctor have massive respect for one another. He's happy to follow her lead, and she relies on his strength and bravery.

◆ He thinks she's a bit daft to constantly go looking for trouble!

RYAN

◇ Graham is protective of Ryan and wants to be closer to him. He knows it'll take time, and doesn't complain.

◇ He worries about Ryan, and just wants to keep him safe, like Grace always has.

YAZ

◇ Graham is fond of Yaz, and worries about her picking up the Doctor's dangerous habits!

ANSWERS

PAGE 15
MISSION 1: Match the Fluid Links
A and H are the same.

PAGE 17
MISSION 2: Monster Hunt

PAGE 19
MISSION 3: Swerve the Spiders
Path B

PAGE 23
MISSION 5: The Caves of Androzani

PAGE 25
MISSION 6: Find the Foe
The Rani

PAGE 27
MISSION 7: The Runes of Fenric
The runes spell out: *The Wolves of Fenric shall return for their treasure.*

PAGE 28
MISSION 8: Karn Challenge

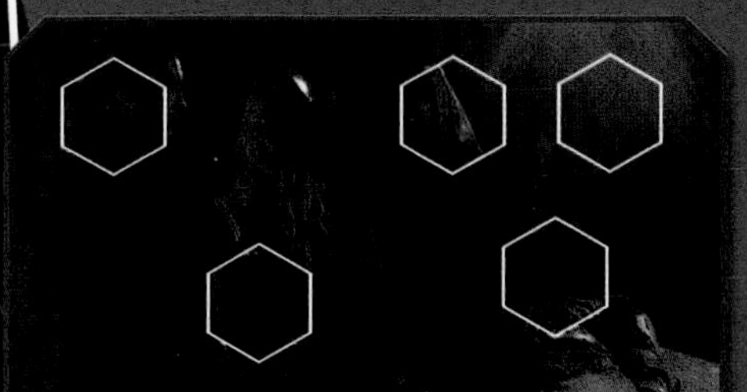

PAGE 29
HIDDEN MISSION: Time War Test
The letters spell out: NO MORE.

PAGE 31
MISSION 9: Bad Wolf
BAD WOLF is written 11 times on the wall.

PAGE 33
MISSION 10: Find the Right Future!
Answer B

PAGE 35
MISSION 11: Don't Blink
Angel E has moved
(The arm has moved)

PAGE 37
MISSION 12:
The Name of the Doctor

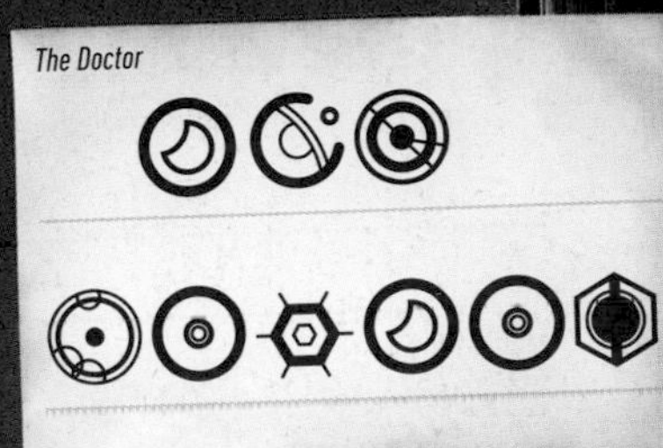

PAGE 56
TARDIS TWINS
C and H are the same.

PAGE 57
TIME TWISTED

You've done it! The Doctor has been saved, and is back in the TARDIS with her friends, sorting out fair play across the universe!

But your mission isn't over! The Doctor has loads of adventures to come, and you can join her on all of them.

START BELIEVING!